the CRitteR club

Amy on Park Patrol

by Callie Barkley ♥ illustrated by Tracy Bishop

LITTLE SIMON

New York London Toronto Sydney New Delhi

LITTLE SIMON

An imprint of Simon & Schuster Children's Publishing Division · 1230 Avenue of the Americas, New York, New York 10020 · First Little Simon hardcover edition May 2017 Copyright © 2017 by Simon & Schuster, Inc. All rights reserved, including the right of reproduction in whole or in part in any form. LITTLE SIMON is a registered trademark of Simon & Schuster, Inc., and associated colophon is a trademark of Simon & Schuster, Inc. For information about special discounts for bulk purchases, please contact Simon & Schuster Special Sales at 1-866-506-1949 or business@simonandschuster.com. The Simon & Schuster Speakers Bureau can bring authors to your live event. For more information or to book an event contact the Simon & Schuster Speakers Bureau at 1-866-248-3049 or visit our website at www.simonspeakers.com.

Designed by Laura Roode · The text of this book was set in ITC Stone Informal Std.

Manufactured in the United States of America 0417 MTN

10 9 8 7 6 5 4 3 2 1

Cataloging-in-Publication Data for this title is available from the Library of Congress.

ISBN 978-1-4814-9433-5 (hc)

ISBN 978-1-4814-9432-8 (pbk)

ISBN 978-1-4814-9434-2 (eBook)

Table of Contents

Chapter 1   Amy on Park Patrol 1

Chapter 2   Growing Doubts 13

Chapter 3   Tiny Workers, Big Job 23

Chapter 4   Pollinator Party 33

Chapter 5   Name That Flower! 47

Chapter 6   Sign Here 53

Chapter 7   Interest from Someone Interesting 63

Chapter 8   The *Sting* of Defeat 77

Chapter 9   Hummingbird Central 87

Chapter 10   A Surprise for Amy 97

Amy on Park Patrol

Amy Purvis spotted an empty plastic water bottle under a tree.

"Found another one!" she called out. She picked it up and put it in her recycling bag.

Amy was volunteering with Park Patrol, a group that cleaned up the Santa Vista Town Park. They met there one Saturday a month. Then they split up into teams to cover different areas.

Another volunteer on Amy's team, Kayla, had a bag for trash.

Jonah had a bag for food waste, like banana peels and apple cores. They would go in the park compost heap.

Amy was in charge of the recycling bag. So far she had found ten empty bottles and cans. The group leader, Mr. Schultz, would turn them in for the bottle deposit. The money would buy more bags and other cleanup supplies.

When the team was done with their rounds, they all gathered around Mr. Schultz.

"Great work, everyone!" said Mr. Schultz.

Amy smiled proudly. She knew lots of wild animals lived in the park, like birds, squirrels, groundhogs, and foxes, so it was important to keep it clean. That morning, her team had even seen a duck nest by the pond. Those baby ducks could have gotten sick from eating people's trash!

Amy checked her watch. It was almost time for her to meet Ellie, Liz, and Marion over at The Critter Club. That was the animal rescue shelter they ran together in their friend Ms. Sullivan's barn.

"Sorry! I have to leave a little early," Amy told Mr. Schultz. "I'll see you next month."

"Okay. Thank you, Amy," said Mr. Schultz. "Next month we'll meet at the other end of the park. There will be some construction starting at this end."

"Construction?" said Jonah.

Mr. Schultz nodded. "The town has decided to build some stores here."

Amy was confused. "But Santa Vista has lots of stores already," she said. "We only have *one* town park."

"What kind of stores?" a boy named Liam asked.

"I don't know much," said Mr. Schultz. "But I've heard that there will be a health-food store, a frozen yogurt shop, and a bookstore, plus others." He sighed. "At least most of the park will still be here."

Amy froze. Had Mr. Shultz said "bookstore"?

She *loved* bookstores. The hushed voices and swoosh of turning pages. The smell of brand-new books. Plus, there were sometimes books at the bookstore that the library didn't even have yet.

And this section of the park *was* kind of wild. It didn't have bike paths or playgrounds or picnic areas. But to Amy, that's what was beautiful about it.

Amy didn't know what to think about this news.

Was it good . . . or bad?

Growing Doubts

Amy's mom gave her a ride over to The Critter Club. She found Ellie, Liz, and Marion in Ms. Sullivan's garden.

They didn't have any animal guests to take care of, so the girls had offered to help Ms. Sullivan plant some flowers. She had a brand-new hummingbird feeder. But so far, no

hummingbirds had come to use it.

Ms. Sullivan had bought some flowers to plant around the feeder. She hoped it would help attract the birds.

The girls took a break from dig-
ging holes as Amy shared the news
about the park.

"Mr. Schultz said there would
be a bookstore. And then on the
ride over here, my mom told me it's
going to be a *children's* bookstore,"

Amy said, staring dreamily into the distance. *A whole bookstore filled with kids' books!*

"Won't all those new stores make the park smaller?" Liz asked.

"Yes. But it *is* a part of the park

that people don't use very much,"
Amy said timidly. She still wasn't
sure that was a good reason to get
rid of it. "Maybe a new bookstore
will get kids excited to read!" Amy
added.

Ellie, Liz, and Marion nodded.

"But why do they have to build
it *there*?" Marion wondered.

That was the big question. And
Amy did not have a good answer.

The girls continued to work in the garden. They planted red lobelia, California fuchsia, and three different kinds of sage.

As Ellie patted the soil around

the last flower, Ms. Sullivan came out to check on their progress.

"Beautiful!" she cried. "Thanks for your help, girls. If I were a hummingbird, this is where I'd want to be. I hope they will come and find it."

"Maybe they'll decide to build a nest nearby," Marion said.

Nest. Amy thought about that duck nest in the park.

Then she gasped as she realized something. To build the stores, they'd have to cut down trees and clear out bushes.

What about all the animals that lived there?

What would happen to all the ducks and squirrels and ground-hogs and foxes?

Chapter 3

Tiny Workers, Big Job

At school on Monday, Amy was still thinking about the park. She, Ellie, Liz, and Marion had agreed: They wanted to do something to stop the construction.

But what?

Amy sighed and turned her mind to schoolwork. Mrs. Sienna was starting the science lesson.

"Today we're going to find out how flowering plants make seeds through a process called *pollination*," Mrs. Sienna said. "That's when pollen from one flower gets inside of another. But how? Plants can't just move from place to place!"

The class laughed. Amy pictured a daisy walking through a garden carrying a suitcase full of pollen.

Mrs. Sienna asked the class to line up by the classroom door. "We're going out to make some observations!" she said.

She led them outside to a flower bed near the playground.

"What if I told you some of these flowers are being pollinated right now?" Mrs. Sienna said. "How? Let's

see if we can solve this mystery."

Amy perked up. She loved a good mystery!

"How could pollen be moving from flower to flower?" Mrs. Sienna asked.

A breeze blew across the playground. Some of the flowers leaned to one side.

Liz raised her hand.

"Does wind move pollen?" she asked.

Mrs. Sienna's eyebrows went up. "Interesting!" she replied. "Yes. Wind can carry pollen through the air. Any other ideas?"

Amy leaned in to study a lilac up close. She took a big whiff of its strong perfume. *Mmmmm.*

Suddenly, Amy pulled back.

Buzzzzzzz. A bumblebee had landed on the flower. As it crawled around, Amy could see flecks of powder on the bee's hairy back.

She looked around. There were lots of bees flying here and there, landing on the flowers. Amy spotted a few butterflies, too, doing the same.

"The insects?" Amy guessed. "Are they moving the pollen?"

Mrs. Sienna gave Amy a thumbs-up. "Yes!" she exclaimed. "And they don't even know it!"

She explained that the insects were just looking for food—the sweet nectar inside the flower. But as they did this, pollen got stuck on their bodies. Then, when they visited the next flower, some of the pollen shook loose.

"Ta-da!" Mrs. Sienna said. "That's pollination! These insects are *pollinators*. They are doing a very big job. Without pollinators, these plants couldn't make seeds. And without seeds, we wouldn't have these flowers!"

Next to Amy, Ellie gasped. "No flowers?!" she cried. "What a nightmare!"

Amy laughed. Ellie was always so dramatic.

But one thing was for sure. Pollinators were teeny-tiny heroes!

Chapter 4

Pollinator Party

"Are we almost there?" Marion asked. She shifted the heavy picnic basket from one arm to the other.

"Here, let me help," said Liz. She took one handle while Marion kept hold of the other.

The girls were tromping through the town park. Ellie carried a big water bottle and cups. Amy led the way, a picnic blanket tucked under her arm.

"There's a good spot just ahead!" Amy called back.

This after-school picnic had been Amy's idea. She thought it would be good to know more about the part of the park they were trying to save.

Finally, Amy stopped. She spread out the blanket in a grassy clearing. Golden sunlight shone down on clusters of wildflowers.

"I've never been back here before," Liz said.

"Me neither," said Ellie. "It's so pretty."

"And so quiet," Marion added.

Amy nodded. "I come back here with Park Patrol," she told them. "I think it's one of the most beautiful parts of the park."

They unpacked the basket and passed out snacks. Marion had brought sandwiches, Ellie had brought fruit, Liz had brought oatmeal cookies, and Amy had brought pretzels and drinks.

They chatted about the school day as they ate. When they were done, they sprawled on the blanket and gazed up at the sky. They played

the Cloud Game, trying to pick out shapes in the cloud patterns.

Eventually, they just lay there listening to the sounds of nature around them.

Marion pulled a notebook from the basket. "I'm going to make a list of all the animals we see. Or hear!" she told them.

"Great idea!" Amy exclaimed. "Then we'll know what sorts of animals and insects live here."

Marion started by writing down the animals they'd seen on the way.

· squirrels
· rabbits
· ducks

"I've definitely seen foxes around here before," said Amy.

Marion added foxes to the list.

They were quiet for a minute, waiting and listening.

A chipmunk scurried out of a hollow log at the edge of the clearing. Ellie pointed at it.

Marion wrote it down.

A bird soared high overhead. "I think that's a crow," Liz said.

Marion added it to the list.

A butterfly flitted past Amy's nose. It circled around Liz's head, over Ellie's knee, and landed for a moment on Marion's notebook.

Marion laughed. "Okay, butterfly! You can be on the list too!"

The butterfly took off again, flying to some tall pink flowers a few yards away. It landed there and sat opening and closing its wings.

Moments later, a loud bumblebee buzzed by.

"Bee!" Marion cried, writing it down. "Got it."

The bee chased the butterfly off the pink flower. It crawled all over, taking time to peek into each bud. Other bees joined. Soon there were four bees buzzing around the same flower.

"What kind of flower *is* that?" Liz asked. "All the pollinators seem to love it!"

Just then an enormous insect swooped in, chasing all the bees away.

In the blink of an eye, it was gone!

"Whoa!" Amy cried. "What *was* that?"

With whirring wings, it suddenly returned. A flash of green rocketed toward the flower, then stopped, hovering in midair.

Finally, Amy could see it clearly. She gasped. It wasn't an insect at all. It was . . .

"A hummingbird!"

Chapter 5

Name That Flower!

Ms. Sullivan studied Liz's drawing of the flower the hummingbird was hovering over.

"You should have seen it, Ms. Sullivan!" Ellie cried. "The hummingbird kept coming back to this flower."

Amy nodded. "It really seemed to like it!"

"So did the bees," added Liz.

"And the butterflies," Marion said.

"Hmm," said Ms. Sullivan. "Let's see." She flipped through her *Wildflowers of California* field guide. Each page had a full color photo of a different flower. "It does look familiar," she added.

Ms. Sullivan turned another page and—

"Stop!" all the girls said at once.

"That's it!" Amy cried.

"'Milkweed,'" Ms. Sullivan read from the book. "I think they had some for sale at the plant nursery.

But it has pink flowers. And I thought hummingbirds liked red flowers best."

Marion read over Ms. Sullivan's shoulder. "It says here they love milkweed. And it's an important plant for Monarch butterflies, too. They lay their eggs on it. When the caterpillars hatch, they eat the milkweed leaves."

"'Many kinds of bees love milkweed nectar,'" Liz read aloud.

They looked up from the book.

"I think I should plant some milkweed!" Ms. Sullivan said.

"It sounds like an important plant," Amy said. "And we saw *so* much of it in that part of the park."

She felt a knot tighten in her stomach.

It was another thing that was going to be lost if they didn't protect the park!

Chapter 6

Sign Here

Marion arrived at school the next day with a piece of paper. She showed it to Amy, Ellie, and Liz at lunch.

Across the top in big letters it read: SAVE THE MILKWEED.

Marion had made it the night before. "This is a petition," she explained.

"It looks great!" Amy told her.

"So official." Ellie nodded with approval.

"Let's see if we can get a bunch of kids to sign it at recess," Liz suggested.

"Okay!" said Marion. She'd even made copies of the petition and brought clipboards and pens.

On the playground, the girls went up to some kids on the swing set. Amy didn't love making speeches, so she was glad when Liz dove right in.

"WHO WANTS TO SIGN OUR PETITION?" Liz shouted.

"Petition?" Joey replied as he swung. "Petition for what?"

"To protect the park," Ellie said.

"And save the milkweed!" Amy chimed in.

Joey frowned. "Milkweed?" he said suspiciously. "You mean ragweed? That makes me sneeze a lot."

Marion shook her head. "No, not ragweed," she said. "*Milk*weed. It's an important plant for lots of insects."

"Cool! I like insects," said Joey. He signed the petition.

But no one else seemed to be listening. They kept on playing.

So the girls walked over to the kids who were playing Four Square. Liz explained what the petition was for.

A few second and third graders signed it. After handing the pen back, one of them said, "Wait. Does this mean they *wouldn't* build the yogurt store?"

Amy nodded. "Right. Or they'd build it somewhere else."

The girl asked for the pen back and crossed out her name. "I *want* them to build it there," she said. "It

would be so close to my house!"

A boy overheard and crossed out his name too. "I like frozen yogurt," he said with a shrug. "Sorry."

The kids went back to their Four Square game.

Ellie sighed in frustration. "There are at least three other yogurt places in town, you know!" she called after them.

The girls tried talking to the kids who were on the playscape. One of them came down to read the petition.

"Weeds?" she said. "I thought weeds were plants that people *wanted* to get rid of."

Amy tried to explain that this weed was a good type of weed.

The girl didn't sign.

By the end of recess, they only had seven signatures—and four were their own.

"This isn't working," Amy said gloomily.

Saving the milkweed was going to be a lot harder than she'd thought.

Interest from Someone Interesting

On Friday the girls met up in the park after school. They had their clipboards. They were trying to get more signatures for the petition.

The girls had come ready with lots of important facts to share with people.

Liz stopped a man pushing his baby in a stroller. "Did you know

that milkweed is an important food for many pollinators?" she asked him.

Marion waved down a cyclist on the path. "Did you know that about seventy-five percent of flowering plants need the help of animal pollinators?" she asked the woman.

Amy went up to parents watching their kids' soccer practice. "Did you know that bee populations are falling?" she asked them.

Some of the people didn't sign the petition. "My grandson is allergic to bees," an older man said.

"Why would I want *more* of them in the park?"

But many of them *did* sign. "Yes!" one woman said. "We have to protect our pollinators!"

The girls had collected about thirty signatures by the end of the day.

"Not bad," said Amy.

"We can try to get more over the weekend."

The girls agreed and headed toward their bikes at the bike rack.

As they walked, they passed a woman walking her dog.

"Excuse me, ma'am," Ellie said to her.

The woman stopped. She listened politely as Ellie showed her the petition. "We're trying to stop the construction in the park," she said. "Would you like to sign?"

"'Save the milkweed,' huh?" the woman read.

Marion jumped in to explain why milkweed was such an important plant.

Liz added that part of the park had lots of milkweed growing in it.

"If the milkweed is cleared out to build stores," Amy said, "the pollinators who need it might not survive."

The woman seemed very interested. She listened carefully to every word. Then she nodded.

"I'd love to see this milkweed for

myself!" she told the girls. "Could you show me?"

The girls looked at one another in surprise.

"Sure!" said Amy. "Right this way!"

The girls turned and led the woman and her dog down the path,

across a footbridge, and through the trees. They even passed by the spot where they'd had their picnic.

Along the way, the girls introduced themselves—first Ellie, then Marion, Liz, and Amy. "We go to Santa Vista Elementary," Amy added.

"Pleased to meet you," the woman replied. "My name is Martha Gomez. I know some of the teachers at SVE!"

Martha Gomez? thought Amy. *That name rings a bell.* Amy didn't recognize her, but then again, she

did see lots of names when she
helped do the filing at her mom's
vet clinic. Maybe this woman took
her dog there?

"Do you know Mrs. Sienna?"
Ellie asked suddenly.

"Ruth Sienna? Yes, I do!" the woman said.

Amy was surprised to hear Mrs. Sienna's full name and even *more* surprised that this woman knew her. "Are you a teacher too, Mrs. Gomez?" she asked.

The woman smiled and shook her head. "I'm not. But I'll give you a hint: Instead of *Mrs.* Gomez, many people call me *Mayor* Gomez."

"Mayor?" said Marion.

The woman nodded. "I'm the mayor of Santa Vista," she said.

chapter 8

The *Sting* of Defeat

For a moment Amy was too shocked to speak.

They were talking to the *mayor?* She had never met a mayor before.

But Mayor Gomez seemed like just a regular person, out walking her dog. And she seemed like a *nice,* regular person.

"I'm very impressed by you all

and your petition," the mayor was saying. "This is clearly an issue you care about very much. When the town council voted to build those stores here, I was all for it. But I want to understand your objections."

They reached the clearing where the girls had first noticed the milkweed.

"Here it is," said Liz, pointing out the milkweed patch.

It was just as busy as it had been the other day. Bumblebees, wasps, and butterflies circled the pink blooms. Luckily, there were plenty of flowers to go around.

"It really is growing everywhere, isn't it?" the mayor said. She moved closer to one of the flowers. "I can see why they like it. It's beautiful, and it smells lovely too."

Amy smiled at Ellie, Liz, and Marion. The mayor seemed to be getting their message.

And if the *mayor* agreed with them, maybe they truly *could* save the milkweed!

"We have thirty-seven signa-tures so far," Marion said, holding up the petition. "And we're going to try to get more."

Mayor Gomez nodded. "Well,

girls," she said. "I admit I did not know very much about milkweed. I've learned a lot today."

A yellow jacket buzzed over from one of the flowers. It circled the mayor's head. She gently waved at it and kept talking.

"I will bring this up with the town council. I think we might need to reconsider—OW!"

The mayor winced and covered her ear with one hand. The yellow jacket flew away.

"Oh no!" cried Ellie. "A bee sting! Are you okay?"

Suddenly, Mayor Gomez's dog started barking at all the insects flying around.

"I'll be all right," the mayor said, rubbing her ear. "But I think we'd better go. Come on, Charlie." She gave her dog's leash a tug and they hurried away.

In a matter of seconds, she was gone.

Amy groaned. "Oh no. That was going so well," she said.

Was the mayor going to want to save the milkweed *now*?

Hummingbird Central

Amy took another bite of her cereal. Across the table, her mom held the Saturday paper open as she read to herself. On the back page was an ad for a chain of children's bookstores.

Ugh, thought Amy. She could hardly stand to think of it—all those milkweed plants, just gone.

"Mom?" Amy said. "Could we

plant some milkweed in our backyard?" If she couldn't save the milkweed in the park, at least she could
plant more.

"Of course we can, sweetheart,"
Amy's mom replied. She peeked
over the top of the paper. "But don't

give up on your petition. You and the girls can get more signatures."

Amy sighed. She knew her mom was right; she shouldn't give up. But getting signatures was going so slowly. By the time they had enough, it might be too late!

It made Amy feel better to visit Ms. Sullivan's hummingbird feeder. She and Ellie, Liz, and Marion stopped by there on Sunday morning.

"Since I planted the milkweed,

it's been nonstop hummingbirds!"
Ms. Sullivan reported.

They were all sitting out on her
back patio. They kept their eyes
glued to the feeder, hoping a hummingbird would pay a visit.

They did not have to wait long.
A tiny bird zipped out of a nearby
tree and rocketed toward the feeder.

"Whoa," the girls all whispered.

They watched as the bird hovered inches from the feeder perch. Its wings beat so fast they were a blur. Without landing, the bird stuck its beak into the feeder.

That's when a second humming-bird dove out of the sky. The first bird darted away, back to the tree. The second bird took sips from the feeder. It moved to the milkweed. It visited all the flowers one by one.

Then the first bird returned from the tree. It joined the other bird in the milkweed.

"Two at the same time!" Ms. Sullivan whispered. "They seem to like the feeder. But they *love* the milkweed."

"Mom and I are going to plant some in our backyard," Amy whispered. She looked at Ellie, Liz, and Marion. "Hey, maybe you three want to plant some, too? If everyone planted a little bit . . ."

Amy's voice trailed off.

Then she stood up suddenly. The startled hummingbirds flew away.

"Oh! Sorry, birds!" Amy called after them. She hadn't meant to scare them off. But she had an idea. "If we can't save the milkweed in the park," Amy began, "maybe we can do the next best thing."

"Yes!" Ellie cried out enthusiastically. Then she frowned. She leaned toward Amy. "What *is* the next best thing?"

"Maybe," Amy said, "we can get everyone to plant milkweed!"

Chapter 10

A Surprise for Amy

The next morning Amy got to school early. She headed for the principal's office. Ellie, Liz, and Marion were going to meet her there. They wanted to talk to the principal, Mrs. Young, about their idea.

Inside the office, the waiting chairs were all empty. *Guess I'm the first one,* Amy thought.

Amy knocked on the principal's door.

"Good morning!" said Mrs. Young from her desk. "Can I help you?"

Right away, Amy felt her face turning red. "Oh hello," she replied. Amy always got a little nervous talking to the principal. *But this is*

important! Amy told herself. She took a deep breath.

"Mrs. Young," Amy began, "could we do some planting here at school?"

Mrs. Young's face lit up with a big smile. At the same time, Amy heard the office door open behind her. *Oh, thank goodness*, thought Amy. Her friends had arrived. Without turning to look at them, Amy kept on

talking. She felt like she was off to a good start.

"We'd like to plant something that's good for pollinators," Amy said. "It's a plant called—"

"Milkweed?" said a woman behind Amy.

Amy turned. Her friends were nowhere to be seen.

Instead, standing in the door-way was a woman in a navy-blue suit. Her hair was pulled back and she was wearing red glasses.

Amy almost didn't recognize her . . . until she smiled.

It was Mayor Gomez! She looked so different all dressed up in her work clothes.

"Well, good morning, Mayor Gomez!" Mrs. Young said in surprise. "Welcome to Santa Vista Elementary!"

"Thank you!" the mayor replied. "I'm sorry to just drop in, but—"

The office door opened again. In

walked Liz, Ellie, and Marion. Their
eyes went wide when they saw the
mayor standing there.

"Oh good! You're all here," Mayor
Gomez said. "I've come with some
news that I wanted to share with
you, girls. I remembered you said
you were students here."

"What news?" Ellie asked.

"Well," said the mayor, "I called a special meeting with the town council over the week-end. We talked a lot about milkweed. We did some research. And we came to a decision."

The mayor paused. Amy held her breath. What was she going to say?

"We've found a good spot for the stores in another part of town," Mayor Gomez announced. "The park will stay just as it is—milkweed and all!"

Amy couldn't believe it. This wasn't just *news*—this was *great news*.

"So . . . we're saving the park *and* getting a new bookstore in town?" Amy asked, just to be sure.

"Yes!" Mayor Gomez replied happily.

This was even better than Amy could have imagined!

"Thank you so much, Mayor Gomez!" all the girls exclaimed.

"After that wasp stung you, we thought . . ." Amy trailed off. "Well, we weren't sure how you felt about milkweed!"

The mayor laughed. "My ear still hurts a little bit," she said. "But I know how important pollinators are.

"What I did *not* know is what an important plant we had in our park." The mayor looked around at all the girls. "And I have *you* to thank for teaching me."

The girls beamed.

"And I was wondering," the mayor went on. "Would you four be interested in teaching the rest of Santa Vista?"

A few months later, Amy, Marion, Liz, and Ellie met Mayor Gomez in the park.

There were lots of other people

there too: all the girls' parents, Ms. Sullivan, Mrs. Young, friends from school, a reporter and photographer from the newspaper, and more!

"Welcome!" said Mayor Gomez. "Thank you for joining us for the opening of the Santa Vista Nature Walk!"

Amy, Liz, Marion, and Ellie beamed. After all, they had helped the mayor *create* the nature walk!

First they'd made a list of the
different kinds of plants and trees
that grew in the park. Next they'd
written a short paragraph
about each one.

The mayor had
signs made with
the information the
girls had written.
They put the signs up

MILKWEED

along a new gravel path. It looped around this end of the park, and it was called the Santa Vista Nature Walk!

"Now the people of Santa Vista have a wonderful way to learn about all the plants that grow and all the animals that live here," Mayor Gomez said, "thanks to the girls of The Critter Club: Amy, Ellie, Liz, and Marion."

Everyone clapped. Amy smiled as the photographer took a photo of them next to the brand-new Nature Walk sign for the newspaper.

"Come on, everyone. Let's take the first walk through the Santa Vista Nature Walk together."

They began at sign number one, titled "Milkweed."

The mayor motioned for Amy and The Critter Club girls to lead the way. And they were happy to do so!

Read on for a sneak peek at
the next Critter Club book:

#18

Ellie Steps Up
to the Plate

the CRITTER club

#18

Ellie Steps
Up to the
Plate

by Callie Barkley ❖ illustrated by Tracy Bishop

In the eighteenth Critter Club book, Ellie tries her hand at softball, but it's harder than it looks! Is she meant only for the stage and not the field? And what happens when Ellie goes searching in the woods near the field for a stray ball and finds . . . an injured baby deer?!

If you like The Critter Club, you'll love
the adventures of
SOPHiE MOUSE

If you like **the Critter Club** you'll love **HEiDi HECKELBECK**

the CRitteR club

Join the club!